THE CHESTER
First Recorder Book of
Christmas Tunes

Mary Thompson
Illustrated by Jan McCafferty

This recorder book belongs to:

....

....

Chester Music limited
(a division of Music Sales Limited)
14-15 Berners Street, London W1T 3LJ, UK.

Good King Wenceslas

My Dancing Day

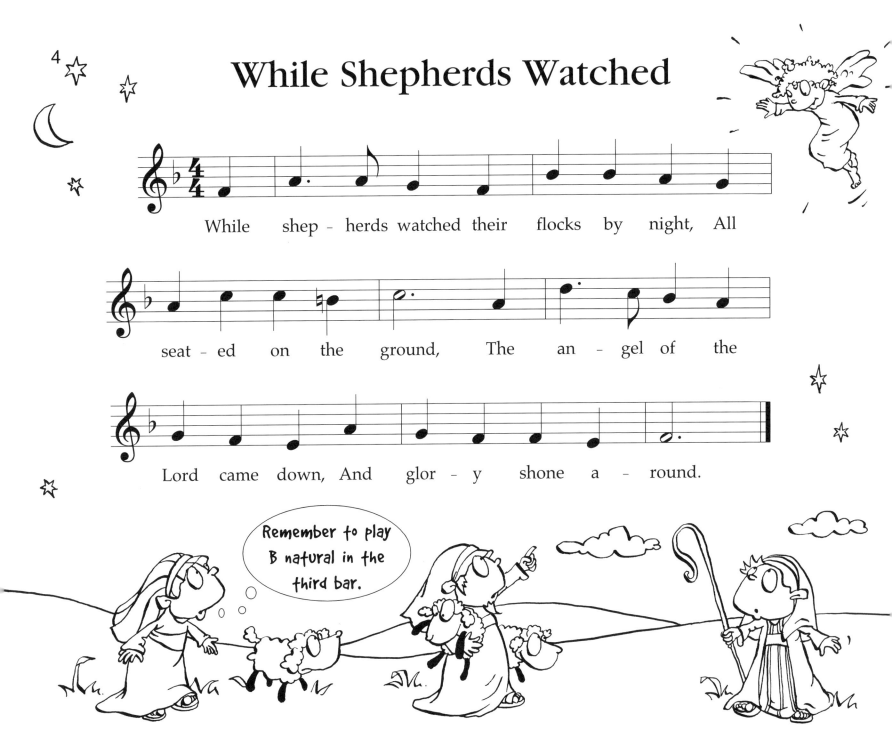

I Saw Three Ships

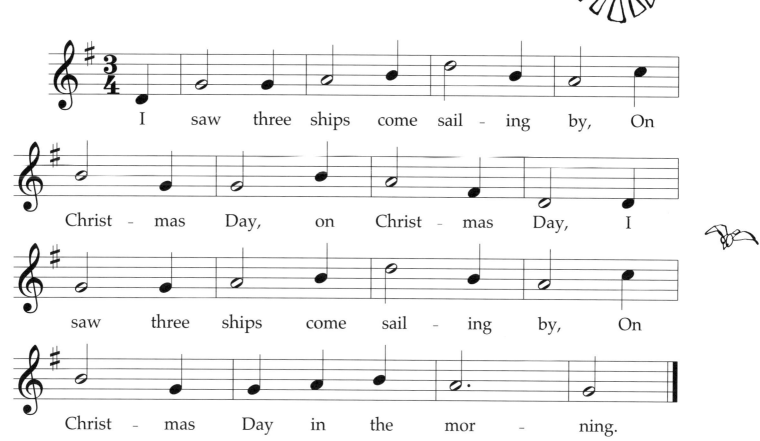

I saw three ships come sail - ing by, On

Christ - mas Day, on Christ - mas Day, I

saw three ships come sail - ing by, On

Christ - mas Day in the mor - ning.

Jingle Bells

Dash-ing through the snow In a one-horse o - pen sleigh,

O'er the fields we go, Laugh-ing all the way;

Bells on bob - tail ring, Mak-ing spi - rits bright; What

fun it is to ride and sing A sleigh-ing song to - night. Oh,

jin - gle bells, jin - gle bells, Jin - gle all the way.

Oh what fun it is to ride In a one-horse o - pen sleigh. Oh,

jin - gle bells, jin - gle bells, Jin - gle all the way.

Oh what fun it is to ride In a one-horse o - pen sleigh.

Unto Us A Boy Is Born

Un - to us a child is born! King of all cre -

- a - tion. Came in - to a world for - lorn, The

Lord of ev - 'ry na - - - - tion.

Away In A Manger

A - way in a__ man - ger, no__ crib for a bed, The__

lit – tle Lord Je - sus lay__ down his sweet head. The

stars in the__ bright sky looked down where he lay, The__

lit – tle Lord Je - sus a - sleep on the hay.

We Wish You A Merry Christmas

Ding Dong! Merrily On High

How Far Is It To Bethlehem

How_ far is it to Beth - le-hem? Not ver - y far. Shall_

we find the sta - ble room Lit by a star? Can

we see the lit - tle child, Is he with - in? If ___

we lift the wood - en latch, May we go in?

Past Three O' Clock

Past three o' - clock, And a cold_ frost-y morn - ing;

Fine

Past three o' - clock, Good mor-row, mas - ters all!

Born is a ba - by, Gen - tle as may be,

D.C. al fine

Son_ of _ the e - ter - nal Fa - ther su - per - nal.

Remember to go back to the beginning and end at the word fine.

God Rest You Merry Gentlemen

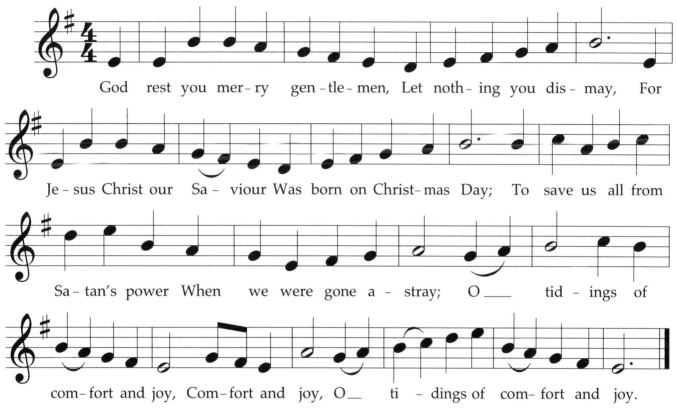

God rest you mer-ry gen-tle-men, Let noth-ing you dis-may, For

Je-sus Christ our Sa-viour Was born on Christ-mas Day; To save us all from

Sa-tan's power When we were gone a-stray; O ___ tid-ings of

com-fort and joy, Com-fort and joy, O__ ti-dings of com-fort and joy.

Once In Royal David's City

Once in roy - al Da - vid's_ ci - ty Stood a

low - ly cat - tle_ shed, Where a moth - er laid_ her_

ba - by, In a man - ger for_ his_ bed. Mar - y

was that moth - er mild, Je - sus Christ her lit - tle_ child.

Hark! The Herald Angels Sing

Rudolph The Red-nosed Reindeer

Ru - dolph the red nosed rein - deer   had a ver - y shin - y   nose,

And if   you ev - er   saw it,   you would ev - en say   it   glows.

All of   the o - ther   rein - deer   used to laugh and call him   names,

They nev - er let poor Ru - dolph   join in a - ny rein - deer games.

Then one fog - gy Christ-mas Eve, San - ta came to say:

"Ru- dolph, with your nose so bright, won't you guide my sleigh to- night."

Then how the rein- deer loved him as they shout-ed out with glee,

"Ru- dolph the red nosed rein-deer, you'll go down in his- tor - y."

We Three Kings Of Orient Are

We three Kings of O-ri-ent are, Bear-ing gifts we trav-el so far,

Field and foun-tain, moor and moun-tain, Fol-low-ing yon-der star. O___

star of won-der, star of night, Star with roy-al beau-ty bright,

West-ward lead-ing, still pro-ceed-ing, Guide us to thy per-fect light.

The Holly And The Ivy

The hol-ly and the i - vy, When they are both full grown, Of_

all the trees that are in the wood, The_ hol-ly bears the crown. The

ris-ing of the sun,_ And the run-ning of the deer, The_

play-ing of the mer-ry or - gan, Sweet sing-ing in the choir.

Silent Night

Deck The Hall

Deck the halls with boughs of hol-ly, Fa la la la la, la la la la,

'Tis the sea-son to be jol-ly, Fa la la la la, la la la la.

Don we now our gay ap-pa-rel, Fa la la, la la la, la la la,

Troll the an-cient Yule-tide car-ol, Fa la la la la, la la la la.

Rudolph The Red Nosed Reindeer

Words and music by Johnny Marks
© Copyright 1949 Saint Nicholas Music Inc, USA.
Warner/Chappell Music Ltd, London W6 8BS.
Used by permission of International Music Publications Ltd.

How Far Is It To Bethlehem

Words by Frances Chesterton
Words reproduced by permission of A.P. Watt Ltd
on behalf of The Royal Literary Fund.

Cover design by Ian Butterworth
Printed and bound in Great Britain by Printwise (Haverhill) Limited.